FOR ELLIE
(MY FELLOW FOOD FIEND)
x

Lino print and collage were used to prepare the full color art.

Published by Sourcebooks Jabberwocky, an imprint of Sourcebooks, Inc.
P.O. Box 4410, Naperville, Illinois 60567-4410
(630) 961-3900
Fax: (630) 961-2168
www.sourcebooks.com

Originally published in 2017 in the United Kingdom by Pan Macmillan, an imprint of Macmillan Publishers Ltd.

Library of Congress Cataloging-in-Publication data is on file with the publisher.

Source of Production: Wing King Tong, Hong Kong
Date of Production: May 2017
Run Number: 5009269

Printed and bound in China.
10 9 8 7 6 5 4 3 2 1

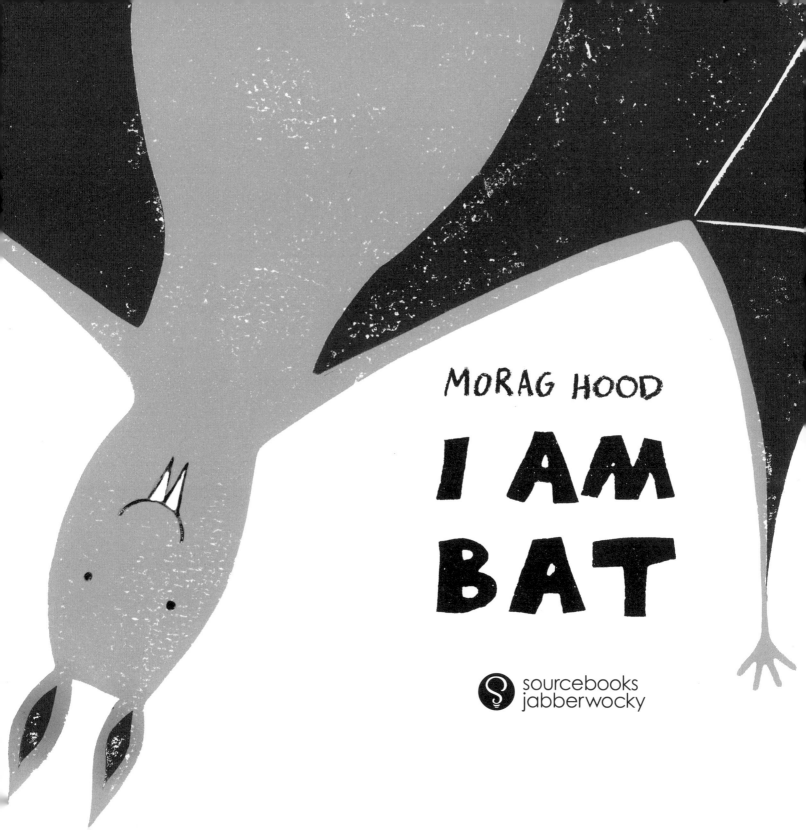

MORAG HOOD

I AM
BAT

sourcebooks
jabberwocky

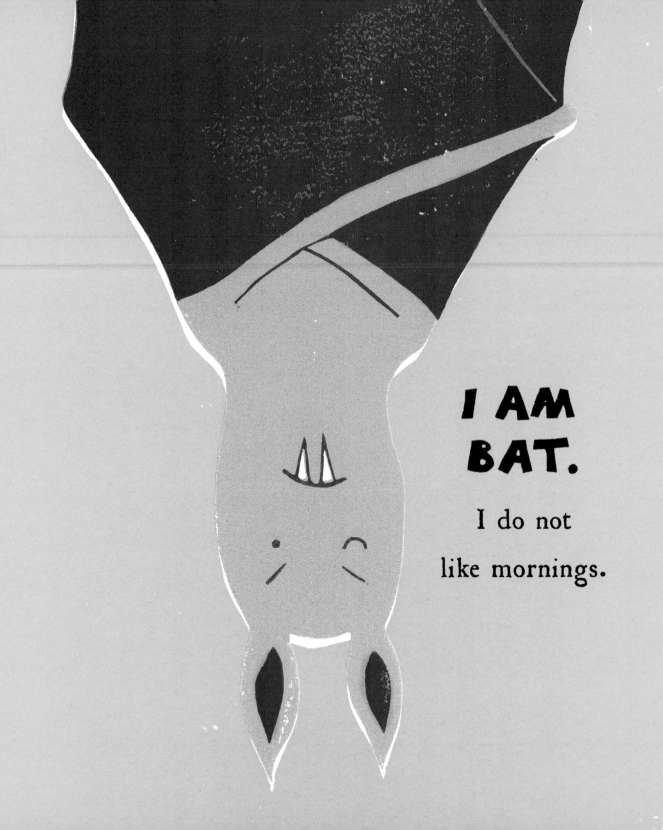

I AM BAT.

I do not like mornings.

I like **CHERRIES.**

They are my

FAVORITE

of all things.

They are

 and

and

DELICIOUS

and...

...THEY ARE MINE.

Do **NOT**

take my cherries.

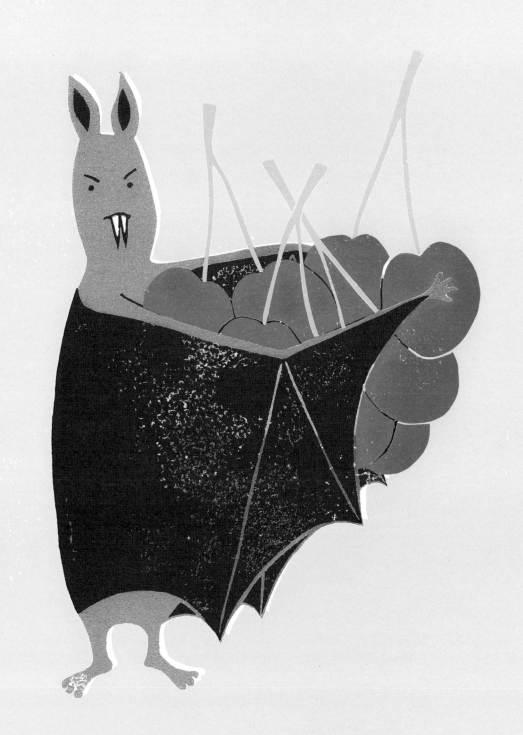

If you take my

cherries

I will be

ANGRY.

I will be **FEROCIOUS** like a lion.

(But smaller and with wings.)

I will just

leave my

cherries

here.

DO

NOT

touch

them.

I WILL KNOW IF
YOU TAKE ONE.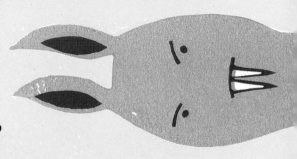

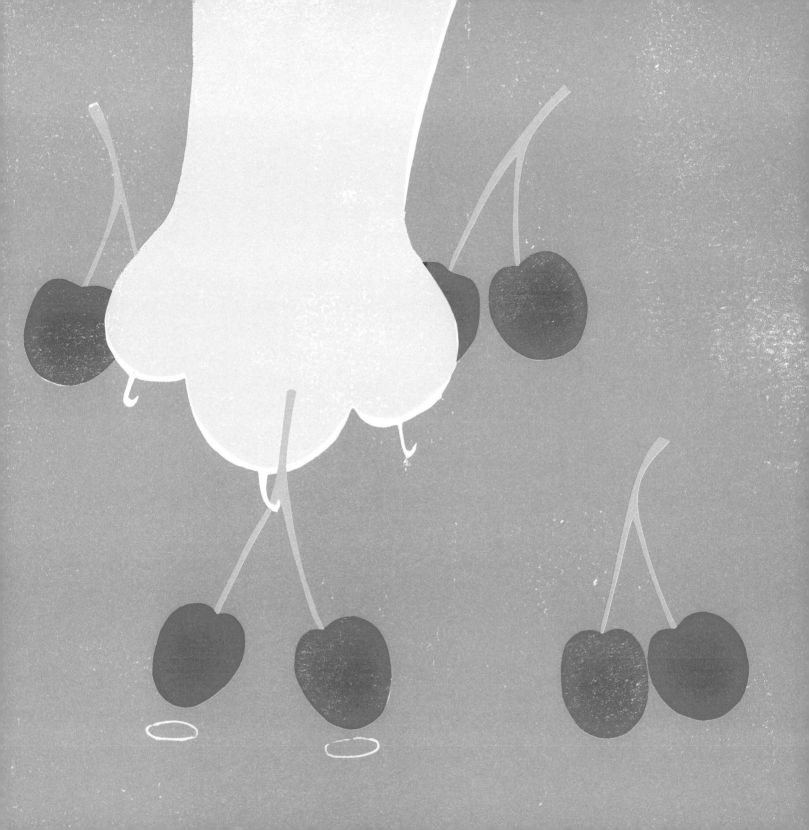

My

CHERRIES!

Some of them are

MISSING.

Where did
they go?

Who stole my

CHERRIES?

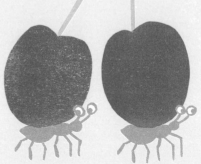

Was it

YOU?

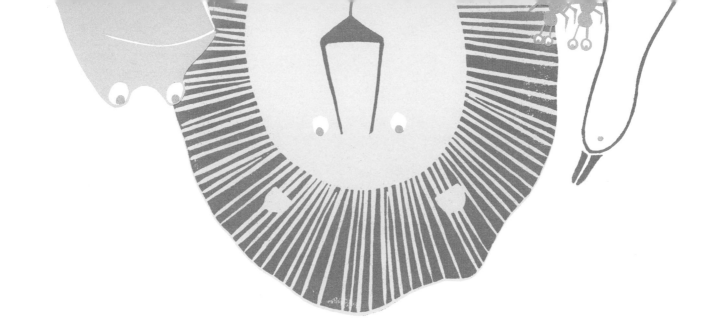

I will

NEVER

be happy again.

Ooh...

A PEAR!

I like PEARS.

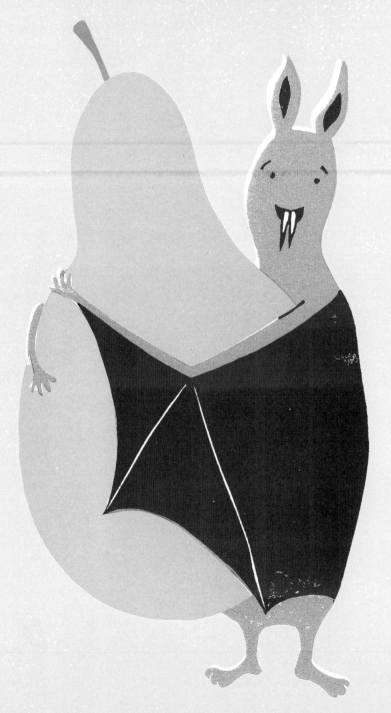

I AM
BAT.

DO
NOT
TAKE
MY
PEAR.